STAR WARS

THE LAST JEDI

™

Read-Along

STORYBOOK AND CD

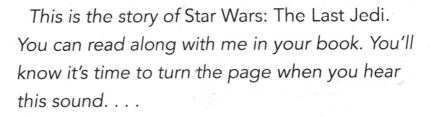

*This is the story of Star Wars: The Last Jedi.
You can read along with me in your book. You'll
know it's time to turn the page when you hear
this sound. . . .*

Let's begin now.

Printed in the United States of America
First Edition, March 2018
1 3 5 7 9 10 8 6 4 2
Library of Congress Control Number on file
FAC-008598-18019
ISBN 978-1-4847-9012-0

Disney
LUCASFILM
PRESS

• LOS ANGELES · NEW YORK •

Certified Chain of Custody
At Least 20% Certified Forest Content
www.sfiprogram.org
SFI-00993
Logo Applies to Text Stock Only

A LONG TIME AGO IN A GALAXY FAR, FAR AWAY,

the Resistance was in trouble.

Resistance fighters had destroyed the First Order's superweapon, the Starkiller, but now the evil group had arrived to seek revenge. The Resistance needed to evacuate its secret base on D'Qar—and fast!

Pilot Poe Dameron found the leader of the Resistance, General Leia Organa, surrounded by advisors on the bridge of the Resistance cruiser. He asked her if he could try to distract the First Order so the remaining Resistance transports could join the rest of the fleet in space.

Leia trusted Poe.

"Permission granted."

Poe leapt into his X-wing with his trusty droid, BB-8, and flew directly toward the largest First Order ship in front of him, a Siege Dreadnought.

"All right, taking out the cannons now!"

Resistance bombers joined the fight, and soon all the Resistance transports had made it to safety. Leia contacted Poe and told him to return to the main cruiser.

"Disengage now, Commander. That is an order!"

But Poe didn't listen. He kept fighting until the Dreadnought was destroyed.

Leia was angry. The Dreadnought had been destroyed and the fleet had jumped to hyperspace to get away from the First Order, but many members of the Resistance had been lost in the attack. Leia knew Poe would be a great leader one day, but he still had a lot to learn.

Poe didn't agree.

"You start an attack, you follow it through."

Just then, former First Order stormtrooper Finn stumbled up to Poe wearing a strange healing bacta suit. Finn had been hurt fighting for the Resistance during the battle on Starkiller Base. He had only one question for Poe.

"Where's Rey?"

Finn's friend Rey had flown to the remote planet of Ahch-To in the *Millennium Falcon* with her Wookiee copilot, Chewbacca, on a special mission for Leia.

Rey was there to convince Leia's brother, the last Jedi Knight, Luke Skywalker, to help the Resistance in the fight against the First Order.

But when Rey offered Luke his old lightsaber, he simply tossed the Jedi weapon carelessly behind him and walked away.

Rey was shocked.

"Master Skywalker?"

Chewbacca saw that Rey needed help, so the Wookiee burst into Luke's hut.

Luke was surprised to see his old friend.

"Chewie . . . what are you doing here?"

Rey and Chewie told Luke about how his former student Kylo Ren was helping the evil Supreme Leader Snoke and his First Order army conquer the galaxy. If Luke didn't come with them or train Rey to become a Jedi, the Resistance—and the galaxy—would be doomed.

"We need your help."

Luke hesitated. He couldn't deny Rey's powerful connection to the Force, but after Kylo had turned to the dark side, Luke never wanted to teach anyone ever again. He was finished with the Jedi Order.

"I only know one truth: it's time for the Jedi to end."

Across the galaxy, the First Order had found a way to track the Resistance fleet through hyperspace.

Kylo Ren led a squadron of TIE fighters on an attack run.

"Follow my lead."

He fired at the main Resistance ship from his TIE silencer, destroying Poe's X-wing and a number of other starships in the hangar bay and blasting a hole in the Mon Calamari cruiser.

Leia was badly hurt in the blast. She was able to save herself only by calling on the Force to pull her to safety. But even with the Force's help, Leia was confined to the medbay and was unable to lead.

Poe thought he might be put in charge, but Leia had left clear instructions that Vice Admiral Holdo was to command the Resistance in Leia's absence.

Holdo and Poe had very different ideas about how to fight the First Order. Poe was itching for action.

"So, what's our plan?"

But Holdo refused to tell him anything.

"Stick to your post and follow my orders."

With Leia unable to lead and the First Order hot on their tail, Finn knew the Resistance was in danger. He decided to leave the fleet to go find Rey. But when he tried to steal an escape pod, he was caught by a Resistance technician named Rose.

"What are you doing here?"

Rose had heard of Finn's heroics during the battle on Starkiller Base and was excited to meet him. However, when she realized that Finn was trying to run away, Rose zapped him with her electro-stun prod and planned to turn him in for desertion.

Finn told Rose the Resistance could not escape the First Order now that the fleet was being tracked through hyperspace. And he was still worried about Rey.

"I'm sorry, but this fleet is doomed, and if my friend comes back to it, she's doomed, too."

But Rose knew that tracking devices could operate only from a single source, meaning that only the First Order's Mega-Destroyer was tracking the Resistance fleet.

With the right

clearance codes, Finn and Rose could sneak on board and disable the tracking device so the Resistance could escape!

Soon Finn, Rose, and BB-8 had zoomed off in a small ship to find a Master Codebreaker to help them infiltrate the Mega-Destroyer.

Back on Ahch-To, Rey refused to give up on Luke.

She followed him all around the island, insisting that he train her or come back with her to help the Resistance.

While Rey and Luke argued, Chewie entertained himself by making friends with the strange creatures called porgs that lived on the island.

The little porgs were curious about the big furry Wookiee. Soon they wouldn't leave him alone!

Meanwhile, Luke had found an old friend on the *Millennium Falcon*.
"Artoo?"
The little droid buzzed angrily at his former master that the Resistance needed his help.

Luke told R2-D2 that nothing could change his mind.

R2 replied by projecting a familiar hologram: young Leia begging for help.

"You're my only hope."

Luke was caught off guard by the hologram that had started his adventures so many years before. He couldn't ignore his sister's words. He decided to give Rey a chance the next morning.

But the next day, Rey saw Kylo Ren standing above her.

She fired her blaster at the dark warrior, but it just put a hole in the wall of her hut.

"You'll bring Luke Skywalker to me."

Rey did not understand why the Force would connect her with Kylo so they could see and hear each other, but she didn't care; she was too mad at him for hurting her friends in the Resistance.

"You're gonna pay for what you did."

Kylo laughed cruelly. He told Rey that Luke was hardly innocent. He accused his old master of trying to hurt him long before Kylo turned to the dark side.

Rey was glad that Luke had agreed to train her, but she could not stop thinking about Kylo's accusation. She did not trust Kylo, but she also sensed conflict in him. She began to hope that he might be brought back to the light side of the Force.

As Rey learned about the Force from Luke and practiced with her lightsaber, she knew she needed to hear the whole story. She needed to ask Luke about what had really happened with Kylo.

Rey gathered her courage and asked Luke about Kylo's claim.

"Is it true?"

The old Jedi shook his head sadly. Luke said that he had never tried to hurt Kylo, but Luke still blamed himself for not saving his young student.

"Snoke had already turned his heart."

That was why Luke had retreated to Ahch-To Island.

Across the galaxy, Finn, Rose, and BB-8 had arrived in the beautiful city of Canto Bight. The wise old alien Maz Kanata had told them they could find a Master Codebreaker there who would help the Resistance.

Finn was impressed by the city's glitz and glamour, and the majestic creatures called fathiers that were raced there for sport.

"This place is *great*!"

But Rose did not like Canto Bight. She knew the wealthy people there had profited off the war between the First Order and the Resistance. They did not care about right or wrong, just as they did not care about the imprisoned fathiers that entertained them.

Unfortunately, before Finn and Rose could find the Master Codebreaker, Canto Bight security found *them*.

Finn and Rose were thrown into jail for crashing their ship on a private beach.

In their cell, a scruffy-looking man named DJ overheard Finn and Rose talking about their mission and said he could easily bust them out of jail and sneak them on board the Mega-Destroyer for the right price.

Finn and Rose were doubtful, but they didn't really have any better options; so while BB-8 provided a distraction, DJ punched a few buttons and opened their cell door.

Finn and Rose were separated from BB-8 and DJ during their escape and stumbled into the fathier stables. They jumped onto one of the creatures and galloped freely through the city streets—crashing into speeders and through the casino.

But on the outskirts of the city, their fathier came to a skidding halt at the edge of a cliff. There was nowhere else for Finn and Rose to go. They said good-bye to the fathier as it ran to its freedom. Just as guards were closing in on them, a shiny sports ship pulled up next to Rose and Finn.

DJ and BB-8 had come to rescue them!

"BB-8! Wait, are you flying that thing?"

Back on Ahch-To, Rey and Kylo's strange Force connection continued. The more time Rey spent talking to her enemy, the more she became convinced that she could save him from the dark side.

Rey reached out to take Kylo's hand, but the moment they touched, Luke witnessed their connection and grew angry. He feared that once again a student of his was being tempted by the dark side.

"Leave this island. Now!"

When Rey refused, Luke drew his staff and tried to force her to leave. Rey believed she could save Kylo—and the galaxy.

"There's still conflict in him. If he were turned from the dark side, that could shift the tide."

Luke disagreed.

"This is not going to go the way you think."

If Luke wouldn't help the Resistance, Rey would have to do it herself.

Sadly, she returned to the *Falcon* and set a course for the Mega-Destroyer, where she knew she would find Kylo.

It was painful for Luke to watch Rey leave; he had lost another student, and it hurt him deeply.

Luke grabbed a torch and walked to the sacred tree where he had kept the last books of Jedi wisdom. If he really wanted the Jedi to end, their knowledge had to be wiped from the galaxy.

But before Luke could burn the books, a bolt of lightning struck the tree, setting it on fire. Without thinking, Luke ran to protect the tree he had almost destroyed himself. Then he heard a familiar voice.

"Pass on what you have learned."

It was Yoda.

The voice of Luke's old teacher filled him with regret. He thought he had been doing the right thing, but Rey's pleas for help echoed in his mind.

Across the galaxy, Finn, Rose, and DJ— disguised as First Order officers—had snuck on board the Mega-Destroyer with BB-8 in tow.

DJ had kept his end of the bargain, cracking the First Order clearance codes so they could get onto the ship and disable the tracking device.

But while Rose and Finn had paid DJ well, it turned out the First Order had paid him better.

DJ betrayed them to Captain Phasma and her elite troopers.

Phasma was not happy to see her former soldier Finn again.

"You were always scum."

Rose and Finn were surrounded by troopers, but their faithful droid, BB-8, once again came to the rescue!

The little astromech took control of a dangerous two-legged walker. Chaos erupted in the Mega-Destroyer's hangar bay, clearing a path for the friends to steal a First Order ship and escape.

In another wing of the Mega-Destroyer, Rey had surrendered herself to Kylo. She told him that when they touched, she had seen his future. He would turn to the light side of the Force.

Kylo shook his head.

The visions he had seen were of Rey's past. He knew her parents were nothing but heartless, penniless scavengers who had left her long before. He believed she would turn to the dark side.

Kylo took Rey before his master, Supreme Leader Snoke.

"Well done, my good and faithful apprentice. My faith in you is restored."

The evil master took Rey's lightsaber from her and examined the powerful weapon while clutching Rey tight in a Force grip.

"For you, all is lost."

But Kylo had a plan of his own.

"I know what I have to do."

While Snoke was distracted, Kylo used the Force to turn Rey's lightsaber so it faced Snoke. In one quick movement, Kylo ignited the weapon, destroying Snoke forever.

Rey was thrilled! She thought Kylo had joined her to fight for what was good and right. But then Kylo raised his lightsaber and pointed it at Rey, and she realized he had destroyed Snoke only to gain more power.

Kylo tried to convince Rey to join him. He even taunted her with his vision of her real parents.

"You have no place in this story. You come from nothing. You're nothing."

Rey struggled to ignore his words. Both she and Kylo reached for her blue lightsaber—Luke's old weapon. It seemed suspended in the air, pulled in two different directions. Rey and Kylo pulled harder and harder, until the lightsaber burst into pieces.

Without a weapon, Rey was defenseless. It seemed that Kylo had won. . . .

Then the room suddenly shook as a Resistance cruiser crashed through the First Order ship!

Vice Admiral Holdo had jumped the Mon Calamari cruiser to hyperspace *through* the Mega-Destroyer! The First Order ship split in two, allowing Rey to escape from Kylo and distracting the First Order while the rest of the Resistance soldiers evacuated to the nearby planet of Crait.

Poe had not understood Holdo's methods, but he would forever respect her sacrifice.

Unfortunately, Kylo Ren, the new Supreme Leader of the First Order, was also able to escape before the ship imploded.

Rose, Finn, and BB-8 rejoined their friends in an old abandoned Rebellion base in a cave on the salt-covered planet of Crait. There the Resistance would make its last stand against the First Order—led by General Leia, who had regained her strength.

"It's now or never."

Resistance pilots ran to old ski speeders, and foot soldiers readied themselves in the trenches. Poe rallied the troops over his comlink.

"Ground forces, lay down some fire!"

An epic battle ensued. With each blast, white salt blew away from the surface of the planet, revealing red crystals beneath.

The Resistance troops were far outnumbered, but they kept fighting.

Suddenly, the *Millennium Falcon* roared into view, with Rey shooting down enemy TIEs and blasting the First Order army.

"Chewie! Peel off from the battle. Draw them away from the speeders!"

The Resistance troops were able to retreat back to the base, but they needed to find a way to escape.

Then Poe spotted strange crystal foxes in the cave.

"Follow me."

The Resistance followed the creatures to the back of the cave, but that only led them to a small opening in the rocks, just large enough for the crystal foxes to slip through.

Poe and his team were trapped.

Then Luke Skywalker appeared outside the cave. Kylo could hardly believe his eyes. He ordered all the First Order ships to fire on his former master.

"More! *More!*"

But when the smoke cleared, Luke still stood in front of the door.

Kylo left his ship to fight the last Jedi himself. The two battled hard. Kylo seethed with anger.

"The Resistance is dead. The war is over."

Luke disagreed.

"The Rebellion is reborn today. The war is just beginning. And I will not be the last Jedi."

Then Kylo struck Luke with his lightsaber, but the Jedi Master simply disappeared.

Luke had never left Ahch-To Island. He had been using the Force all along. And now the Jedi could peacefully become one with the Force.

With Luke distracting Kylo and the First Order, Rey and Chewbacca searched for their friends from outside the cave.

"If the beacon's right beneath us, they've gotta be somewhere. Keep scanning for life-forms!"

Then Rey saw the foxes climbing through the small opening in the rocks and sensed what she needed to do. She quieted her mind, as Luke had taught her, and reached out with the Force.

The passage began to tremble as Rey lifted the massive stones, one by one, up and away from the cave, clearing the opening to free the Resistance troops.

The remaining members of the Resistance crowded onto the *Millennium Falcon*, and the ship zoomed off into hyperspace.

The journey ahead would be difficult. The Resistance needed time to rebuild its strength, and the group shuddered at the thought of what Kylo Ren and the First Order would do next.

But the Resistance had something the First Order could never take away. Together, they had hope—hope that one day they would defeat Kylo Ren and the First Order for good and bring peace to the galaxy once again.